Who Loves Mr Tubs?

For Bebe Waddell
B.M.

For Tamlyn
S.H.

EGMONT
We bring stories to life

First published in Great Britain 2006
by Egmont UK Ltd.
239 Kensington High Street, London W8 6SA
Text copyright © Bel Mooney 2006
Illustrations copyright © Susan Hellard 2006
The author and illustrator have asserted their moral rights.
ISBN 978 1 4052 2304 1
ISBN 1 4052 2304 9
10 9 8 7 6 5 4 3
A CIP catalogue record for this title is available from the British Library.
Printed in Singapore

Bel Mooney Susan Hellard

Who Loves Mr Tubs?

Blue Bananas

Mr Tubs was always pleased on Kitty's birthday, because she was so happy. He liked to see her smile.

Kitty put Mr Tubs down to open her presents. When she came to the parcel from her aunt and uncle and cousin Melissa she had a surprise.

How lovely!

Oh, it's a doll.

You don't really like dolls, do you?

Mr Tubs watched Kitty take her new doll out of the box and hold her up in the air.

Just then Kitty's friends Rosie and
Anita arrived for tea. They loved
Kitty's new toy and both admired her
trendy clothes.

Later, they put Kitty's new CD on and danced around the room. Mum joined in, saying she loved the song.

This is great!

I'm a good dancer.

Ow!

At last it was time for Kitty to go to bed. Suddenly she spotted Mr Tubs on the floor and picked him up. She gave him a big hug and whispered that Suki would be his new best friend.

You'll like Suki, won't you, Mr Tubs?

Yes, Kitty.

I don't think so.

Kitty settled down in bed to read one
of her new books, with Suki on one side
and Mr Tubs on the other.

She said thank you to Mum for a
lovely birthday.

In the middle of the night Mr Tubs

dreamed that he was climbing a tree.

He wanted to find the honeycomb that

the bees had left in the branches.

But just when he got near the honey a

beautiful, bad bird flew at his head.

She sang loudly in his ear,

telling him to

go away.

Go away!

Mmmm –
yummy honey.

Zzzzstop
zzzzstealing,
Mr Tubzzzzzz!

Mr Tubs fell to the ground with a

thump. Suddenly the sun had gone,

and everything was dark . . .

In the morning Kitty was late for school as usual. Rushing around, she didn't notice Mr Tubs on the floor.

Later, Mum came in to make the bed and found Mr Tubs. She put him on the chair with Suki by his side.

The next week, Mr Tubs couldn't

believe it. He sat on the chair . . . and

sat . . . and sat . . . while Kitty took

Suki everywhere.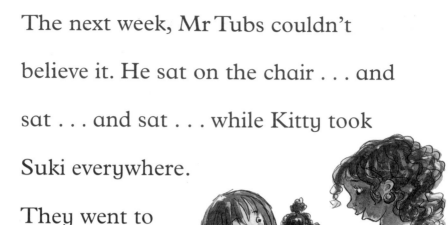

They went to

Rosie's house, and

Rosie's big sister loved the cool doll.

They went shopping for clothes with

Kitty's mum.

They went to the library to

look for a book on dinosaurs.

They met Anita at the ice cream shop.

They watched TV downstairs with

Dan.

All the time Mr Tubs waited,

trying to be brave, feeling

very lonely in Kitty's room.

I don't really mind being on my own.

He could almost feel dust falling

on him, as he waited for Kitty

to take him out again,

like she used to.

Each night Kitty put Suki on the chair next to Mr Tubs, and told them to look after each other. She'd decided that she was old enough to sleep all by herself.

I miss my cuddles with Kitty.

Good - my clothes get all messy in bed.

Each night three different dreams

bobbed about the little bedroom.

One afternoon Baby Tom
just cried and cried.
Mum tried the dummy,
but it didn't work.

She tried the
musical mobile
but it didn't work.

She tried singing a song but Tom just
cried all the more. At last she had to
walk out of the room because she felt
cross and upset and worried –
all at the same time.

She was standing by the door of
Kitty's room when she spotted
Mr Tubs, still waiting on the chair.
Quickly she picked him up and popped
him into Tom's cot.

Now, Tom, look who's come to see you!

Waaaa-
waaaa-
waaaa!

Hurray!
Somebody
wants me!

It really was very noisy in that cot.

Aaaaah-
aaaaah-
aaaaaah!

I've got to do
something
about this.

Tom yelled and yelled right next to

Mr Tubs's ears. And the baby's tears

started to make his old fur all wet.

Nobody really knows how bears can talk to babies. But they can. Mr Tubs started up his most smooth, purring growl, deep inside, and he wished Baby Tom a peaceful sleep with every little bit of his old furry heart.

Later, when Mum tiptoed into his
room to check, Tom was fast asleep,
with one arm round the old bear. She
was very happy.

Oh, Mr
Tubs, you're
so clever.

It's nothing.
Just what us
bears do.

When Kitty came home from school
she went up to her room to fetch Suki.
Right away she noticed Mr Tubs
wasn't in his usual place.

Mum! Have you seen my bear?

Kitty ran all over the house looking for Mr Tubs. Suddenly she felt guilty because she knew she hadn't played with him, and she wanted to put things right.

Mum took her into the baby's room.
Tom was still fast asleep, cuddling
Mr Tubs. Kitty stared into the cot.
Mum said that since she was too
grown-up for her bear, she should
give him to Tom.

I don't want to.
It's not fair.

It is fair!
You always play
with Suki now.

Hello, Kitty.

Kitty pretended she didn't mind. She went into her bedroom and picked up Suki.

Come on, Suki, we'll go and watch TV.

The room seemed empty without Mr Tubs, but Kitty decided not to think about it.

But later, when Kitty tried to make a
den with the sofa cushions like she
used to, Suki didn't look as if she
enjoyed it. Kitty remembered it was
one of Mr Tubs's favourite games.

I wish I had
my bear.

This is really
babyish.

Mr Tubs was quite happy in Tom's cot. It was warm and cosy, and he felt loved. When Mum took the baby downstairs he went too, because Tom loved to hug him – even though he was nearly the same size as him. Mr Tubs felt part of the family again.

Tom loves that teddy!

And at bedtime he liked the songs Mum sang to the baby. Inside his head he joined in. That made him sleepy too.

'Go to sleep now, goodnight, In your bed soft and white,

All the creatures of the day, Must have rest from work and play.'

Mmmmf . . . mmmmf . . . snore.

A few days later Kitty felt ill. She sniffed and snuffled and sneezed so much Mum said she should go to bed. Her nose was red and she felt very sorry for herself. Dad said she would soon feel better.

Kitty went upstairs and put her
pyjamas on.

She looked at her bed and knew she

wanted someone

to cuddle.

I want
Mr Tubs.

No - I'm your
favourite,
Kitty!

She looked at Suki and knew she

wouldn't do. Suki was cool, but

not cuddly.

Kitty crept into Tom's room. He was fast asleep. Mr Tubs lay there, looking up at her. Very carefully she picked him up and held him tight. But just then Tom woke up and started to cry.

Shhhhh.

Mum and Dad came rushing upstairs.

They told Kitty she should leave

Mr Tubs with Tom because the

baby loved him now.

Kitty was very cross.

Kitty rushed into her room, grabbed Suki, and jumped into bed. But her lovely new doll felt hard and cold, and Kitty suddenly knew the truth. She liked Suki but she didn't love her.

So am I, Kitty.

I'm sorry, Suki.

Loving a toy was something that happened over a very long time.

When Mum and Dad came in to see her Kitty tried not to cry. Dad knew what was wrong, and so did Mum. They had to come up with a plan to put it right. But they all knew Tom would be unhappy without the old bear.

So who loves Mr Tubs?

But what about Tom?

I-I do.

Then Kitty had her brilliant idea. Mr Tubs was a bear, but he wasn't the only bear in the world. Even if he was the best bear. Mr Tubs belonged with her. But if she took him back, she must give Tom something in return. The thought made her feel much better.

A couple of days later Kitty was well again. She emptied her money box and put the money in a little pile. Dad said he would take her shopping. She went to say goodbye to Mr Tubs, who was sitting with Tom on Mum's knee.

While they were out Mr Tubs played
with Tom on the floor. They played
'Pull Teddy
Along By The
Ear' and

'Hold Teddy Upside

Down By His Feet'

and 'Pinch

Teddy's Nose'.

Hurry up,
Kitty.

Then Tom laughed and

laughed as he played

'Smack Teddy's Bottom'.

Mr Tubs thought it was all great fun.

But it did make him rather tired.

At last Kitty ran into the room, waving a bag from the toy shop. She pulled out a brand-new bear for Tom. He was smaller than Mr Tubs, and a darker brown with light brown paws.

Look what we've got for Tom!

Oh, what a sweet little bear!

Mr Tubs thought the bear looked very nice. Tom smiled and waved his hands.

Mum told Kitty she must be careful
and not take Mr Tubs back too soon.
So all afternoon she played with Tom
and Mr Tubs. She asked Tom what
they should call the new bear. He
gurgled 'Buh-buh-buh,' and she
clapped her hands. 'Yes!' she cried.
'We'll call him Bubba Bear.'

Mr Tubs and
Bubba will be
best friends,
Tom!

That's a
good name,
Kitty.

Kitty put the two bears on the sofa and went to have her tea. She told Mr Tubs he had to look after Bubba and tell him what to do. Mr Tubs agreed.

You help him, Mr Tubs.

All right, Kitty.

He knew that Bubba might not understand that being a child's bear is really a very important job. He was a rather young bear after all.

Mr Tubs told Bubba all the jobs he had
to do to look after Baby Tom. He made
sure he knew the List of Very
Important Duties of a Teddy.
He had to put up with
getting dirty.

He had to drive away bad dreams
with long, low growls.

He had to make sure Tom
didn't ever feel lonely.

44

He had to be Tom's best friend and

play with him always.

He had to be loyal to Tom and love

him for ever.

Can you remember all that, Bubba?

Bubba listened and said

he would do his best.

Oh, I'll try really hard, Mr Tubs.

When it was Tom's bedtime Kitty put both bears in the cot, but put Tom's arms around Bubba. The little bear looked very happy, and so did Tom. Mr Tubs sang his special soft growly song to help them both get to sleep. Then, very quietly, Kitty took him out of the cot.

Time for you to come home to my room, Mr Tubs.

At last! But what about Suki?

Kitty made a space on the shelf where she kept her favourite books. She picked Suki up and stroked her lovely dark hair. 'You know I really, really like you, Suki,' she said, 'but you're such a special doll I'm going to put you up where I can admire you. Then when Rosie and Anita come to play we'll get you down.'

Everybody can see you up here.

That's my clever Kitty.

Mr Tubs lay on Kitty's pillow. She sat
on the bed and looked at him. 'Can
you forgive me?' she whispered. 'I was
so excited about my new doll that I
forgot about you. But then I realised
how much I missed cuddling you.
I'm soooo sorry, Mr Tubs.'

You know who loves you, Mr Tubs – don't you?

You do, Kitty.

The look in Mr Tubs's black eyes told
her it didn't matter. As long as they
were back together again – for ever.